Dog and Bear

TWO'S COMPANY

Laura Vaccaro Seeger

A NEAL PORTER BOOK
ROARING BROOK PRESS
NEW YORK

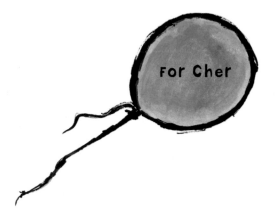

For Cher

A Neal Porter Book

Published by Roaring Brook Press

Roaring Brook Press is a division of Holtzbrinck Publishing Holdings Limited Partnership

175 Fifth Avenue, New York, New York 10010

www.roaringbrookpress.com

Distributed in Canada by H. B. Fenn and Company, Ltd.

Library of Congress Cataloging-in-Publication Data

Seeger, Laura Vaccaro.

Dog and Bear : two's company / Laura Vaccaro Seeger.

v. cm.

"A Neal Porter book."

Contents: Ice cream — Happy birthday Bear! — Sweet dreams.

Summary: Three more easy-to-read stories reveal the close friendship between
a dachshund named Dog and a stuffed bear.

ISBN: 978-1-59643-273-4

[1. Best friends—Fiction. 2. Friendship—Fiction. 3. Dogs—Fiction. 4. Teddy bears—Fiction.] I. Title.

PZ7.S4514Dt 2007   [E]—dc22   2007010038

Roaring Brook Press books are available for special promotions and premiums.
For details, contact: Director of Special Markets, Holtzbrinck Publishers.

Printed in July 2009 in China by South China Printing Co. Ltd., Dongguan City, Guangdong Province

First edition April 2008

2 4 6 8 10 9 7 5 3

"I am very angry with you, Bear.
I am running away."

"All right, Dog. Go ahead."

"I am packing
my bones."

"You do that."

"I am packing my sticks."

"Of course you are," said Bear.

"Don't forget this one," said Bear.

"I am packing all my toys."

"I am packing each and every one of my books," Dog continued.

"That's good. I know how much you enjoy them."

"Goodbye, Bear."

"Goodbye, Dog."

"I suppose you won't be staying for ice cream," said Bear.

"Ice cream?" said Dog. "Well, maybe I'll stay for just a bit."

"I'm glad," said Bear.
"Me too," said Dog.

"Today is Bear's birthday! He will be so surprised!"

"I have baked his favorite birthday cake.
vanilla with strawberry frosting . . ."

"and rainbow sprinkles . . ."

"I can't wait to eat this wonderful cake!
Maybe I could taste a little, tiny bit."

"Mmm. Maybe I could taste
a little, tiny bit more."

"Yummy!"

"oh, no! What have I done?" cried Dog.
"I have eaten all of Bear's birthday cake!"

Just then, Bear walked
into the room.

"Oh, Dog! What a beautiful candle!
You have remembered my birthday!
Thank you!"

"Oh! You're welcome," said Dog.
"Happy birthday, Bear!"

"What's the matter, Dog?"

"I am not feeling well, Bear.
I am very tired."

"Oh, my. Is there anything that I can do to help?" asked Bear.

"Well . . . Maybe you could bring me a cup of tea . . ."

"and a biscuit . . ."

"and a little bowl of soup," Dog continued.

"oh, and perhaps you could
bring me my book . . ."

"and my cozy slippers
and my pillow . . ."

"and . . . maybe my favorite
red blanket," said Dog.

"sweet dreams,
my friend."